TODAY'S HIGH-TECH WEAPONS

NUCLEAR WEAPONS

ALIX WOOD

PowerKiDS press
New York

Published in 2016 by **Rosen Publishing**
29 East 21st Street, New York, NY 10010

Cataloging-in-Publication Data
Wood, Alix.
Nuclear weapons / by Alix Wood.
p. cm. — (Today's high-tech weapons)
Includes index.
ISBN 978-1-5081-4687-2 (pbk.)
ISBN 978-1-5081-4688-9 (6-pack)
ISBN 978-1-5081-4689-6 (library binding)
1. Nuclear weapons — Juvenile literature. 2. Nuclear warfare — Juvenile literature. I. Wood, Alix. II. Title.
U264.W66 2016
355.02'17—d23

Copyright © 2016 Alix Wood Books

All rights reserved. No part of this book may be reproduced in any form without permission in writing from the publisher, except by a reviewer.

Editor: Eloise Macgregor
Designer: Alix Wood
Consultant: Mark Baker

Photo Credits: Cover © Shutterstock/Eky Studio (top), © Shutterstock/optimarc (ctr), © Getty Images/Lonely Planet Images (btm) ; 4 © DoD/Cpl. Lynn P. Walker; 5 © National Nuclear Security Administration; 6 © James E. Westcott; 7 bottom left © United States Department of Energy; 8, 9 © Alix Wood; 10 © Harold Agnew; 11, 15 top © National Government Archives; 12, 17 left, 18 © DoD; 13 © Michael Pereckas; 15 bottom © Charles Levy; 16 © Edward Valachovic; 19 © Diefenbunker; 20 © CBTBO; 21 © NASA/USGS; 23 top © Bob Break; 23 bottom © Smithsonian Institute; 24 © Croquant; 25 top, 26-27 © MoD; 27 top © DoD/Jerry McLain; 27 bottom © Ben Mabbett; 28 © DoD/Sgt. Michael Krieg; 29 © DoD/Raolito M. Pambid; all other images are in the public domain

Manufactured in the United States of America
CPSIA Compliance Information: Batch #BW16PK.
For Further Information contact Rosen Publishing, New York, New York at 1-800-237-9932

CONTENTS

WHAT ARE NUCLEAR WEAPONS?............ 4
THE MANHATTAN PROJECT...................... 6
FISSION AND FUSION 8
HIROSHIMA... 12
THE B-29 BOMBER.................................. 14
NAGASAKI 16
THE COLD WAR 20
BROKEN ARROW 22
TESTING TIMES......................................24
FALLOUT 26
TSAR BOMBA..28
TRIDENT MISSILE 28
NUCLEAR CLEANUP 28
GLOSSARY 30
FOR MORE INFORMATION...................... 31
INDEX 32

WHAT ARE NUCLEAR WEAPONS?

Nuclear weapons are bombs or missiles that use **nuclear energy** to cause an explosion. Nuclear energy is very powerful. Nuclear weapons get their power from the energy released when either a heavy **atom** is divided, called fission, or when light atoms are forced together, called fusion. They are sometimes called atomic weapons.

The force of a nuclear weapon is measured by how much **conventional** explosive would be needed to produce a similar explosion. A kiloton (KT) is a 1,000-ton TNT explosion. A megaton (MT) is a 1-million-ton explosion.

> Nuclear weapons have been used twice in nuclear warfare. Both times were by the U.S. against Japan, near the end of World War II. On August 6, 1945, the U.S. bombed the Japanese city of Hiroshima. Three days later a bomb was dropped over Nagasaki (left). The bombs flattened both cities.

There is concern that nuclear weapons are too powerful. Governments are looking at ways to encourage countries to reduce the amount of nuclear weapons that they have. Another concern is the possibility that **terrorist** groups could buy or develop nuclear weapons.

A nuclear explosion during a test by weapons scientists in 1951

NUCLEAR WEAPON FACT FILE:

WHO WOULD USE THE WEAPONS: Nuclear weapons are expensive so they are mainly held by wealthy countries

CAUSE FOR CONCERN: The weapons can destroy huge areas and kill many thousands of people. If a nuclear war broke out it would lead to large-scale destruction.

PROTECTION AGAINST NUCLEAR WAR: Possessing nuclear weapons makes a country feel safer from other countries that have nuclear weapons. It would be much safer, however, if no one had them!

THE MANHATTAN PROJECT

plutonium

tungsten carbide bricks

On August 21, 1945, at Los Alamos National Laboratory, New Mexico, Harry K. Daghlian accidentally dropped a **tungsten carbide** brick. He was experimenting building a brick reflector around some **plutonium**. The reflector would reduce the amount of plutonium needed for a nuclear chain reaction to occur. As he moved the final brick into place, a warning system alerted him that the last brick would make the plutonium react in a dangerous way. As he quickly pulled his hand away, he accidentally dropped the brick.

A deadly chain reaction began. Daghlian received a lethal dose of **radiation**, and died 25 days later.

WHAT YOU SEE HERE
WHAT YOU DO HERE
WHAT YOU HEAR HERE
WHEN YOU LEAVE HERE
LET IT STAY HERE

The top secret work at Los Alamos was known as the "Manhattan Project." Secrecy was vital. Anyone caught talking about the project would get a 10-year prison sentence!

The Manhattan Project researched and developed nuclear weapons. The project started during World War II, because the Germans were thought to be developing nuclear weapons. The project was headed by J. Robert Oppenheimer, professor of physics at the University of California, Berkeley. Oppenheimer is often called the "father of the atomic bomb" for his role in developing nuclear weapons.

> "Trinity" was the code name of the Manhattan Project's first **detonation** of a nuclear weapon. On July 16, 1945, "The Gadget," as the bomb was called, was dropped from the top of a 100-foot (30 m) steel tower. The height demonstrated how the weapon would behave when dropped from a bomber.

When The Gadget exploded, the shock wave was felt over 100 miles (160 km) away! The mushroom-shaped cloud (below left) was 7.5 miles (12.1 km) high. Below, Oppenheimer (left) and project director Lieutenant General Leslie Groves (right) examine the remains of the steel tower.

FISSION AND FUSION

Nuclear weapons are powered by atomic explosions. The explosion occurs when atoms are split. The enormous energy released by the split causes particles to collide with more and more atoms, creating a chain reaction. This process is called fission. The most powerful fission explosions use **uranium** and plutonium atoms, because they are **unstable** and **radioactive**.

Atomic bombs (also known as A-bombs) produce their explosive energy purely through nuclear fission. Hydrogen bombs (also known as H-bombs) produce energy through nuclear fusion reactions. In nuclear fusion, multiple atoms combine to create a single atom, which releases energy. **Thermonuclear** weapons use both fission and fusion.

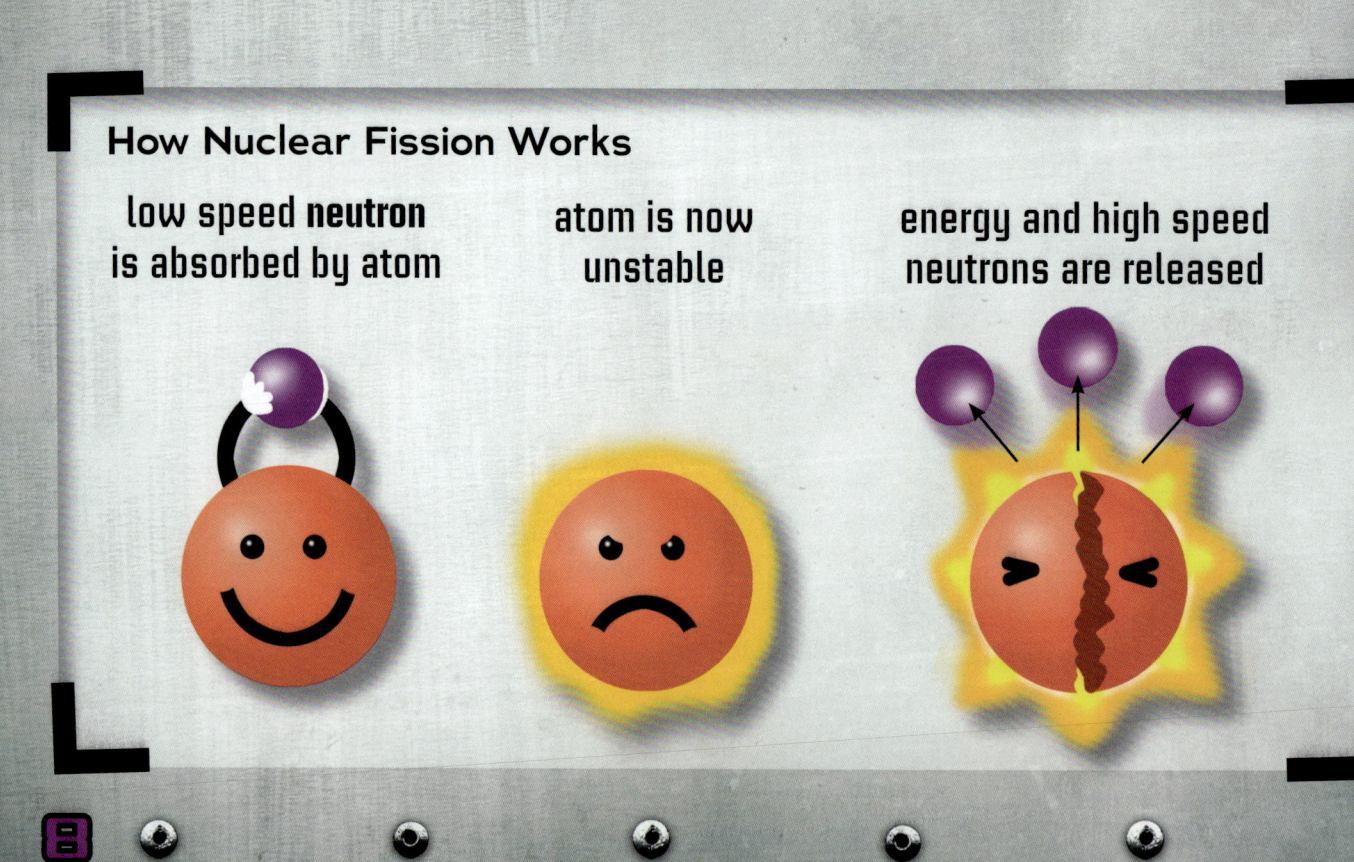

How Nuclear Fission Works

low speed **neutron** is absorbed by atom

atom is now unstable

energy and high speed neutrons are released

How Nuclear Fusion Works

Bombs that use nuclear fusion can be over a thousand times more powerful than ones that use fission.

two small atoms fuse together to form a larger atom

neutron

ENERGY

helium

How a Thermonuclear Weapon Works

FISSION | FUSION
uranium core
neutrons are fired down tube
X-rays
fusion fuel
plutonium | foam | uranium

THERMONUCLEAR WEAPONS FACT FILE:

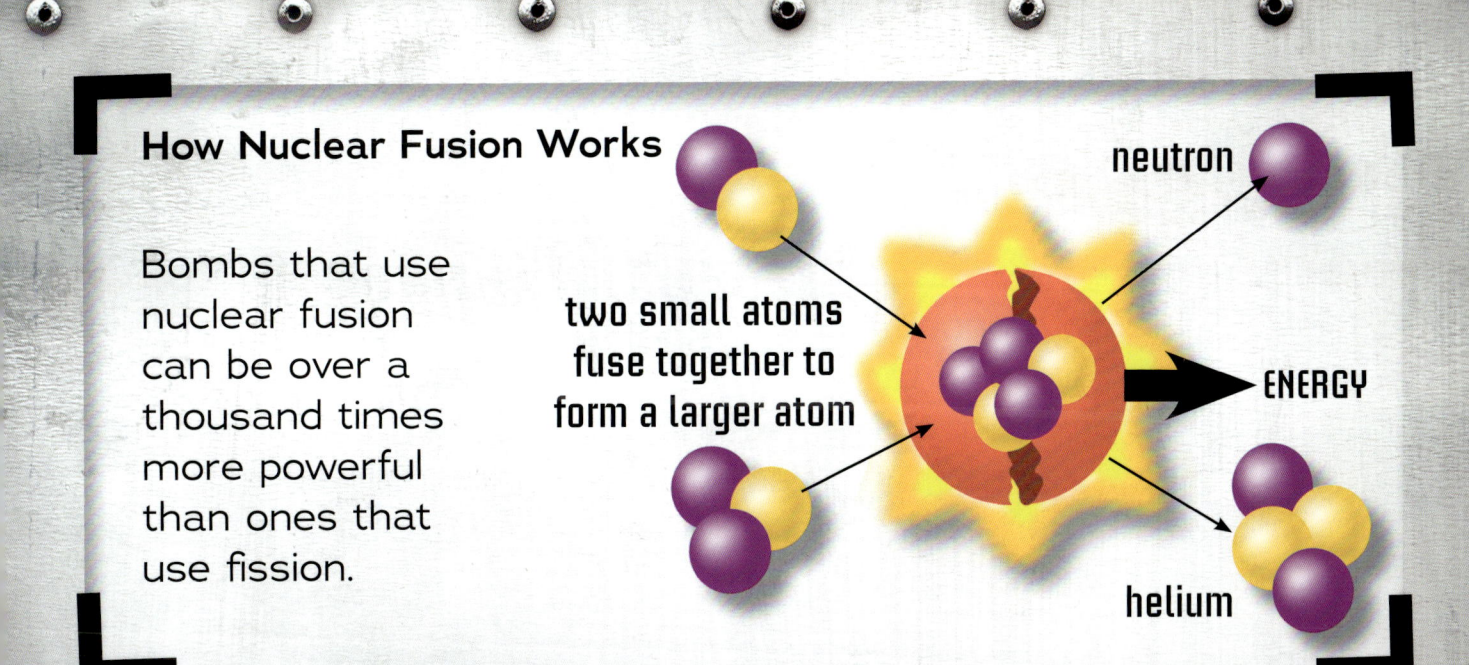

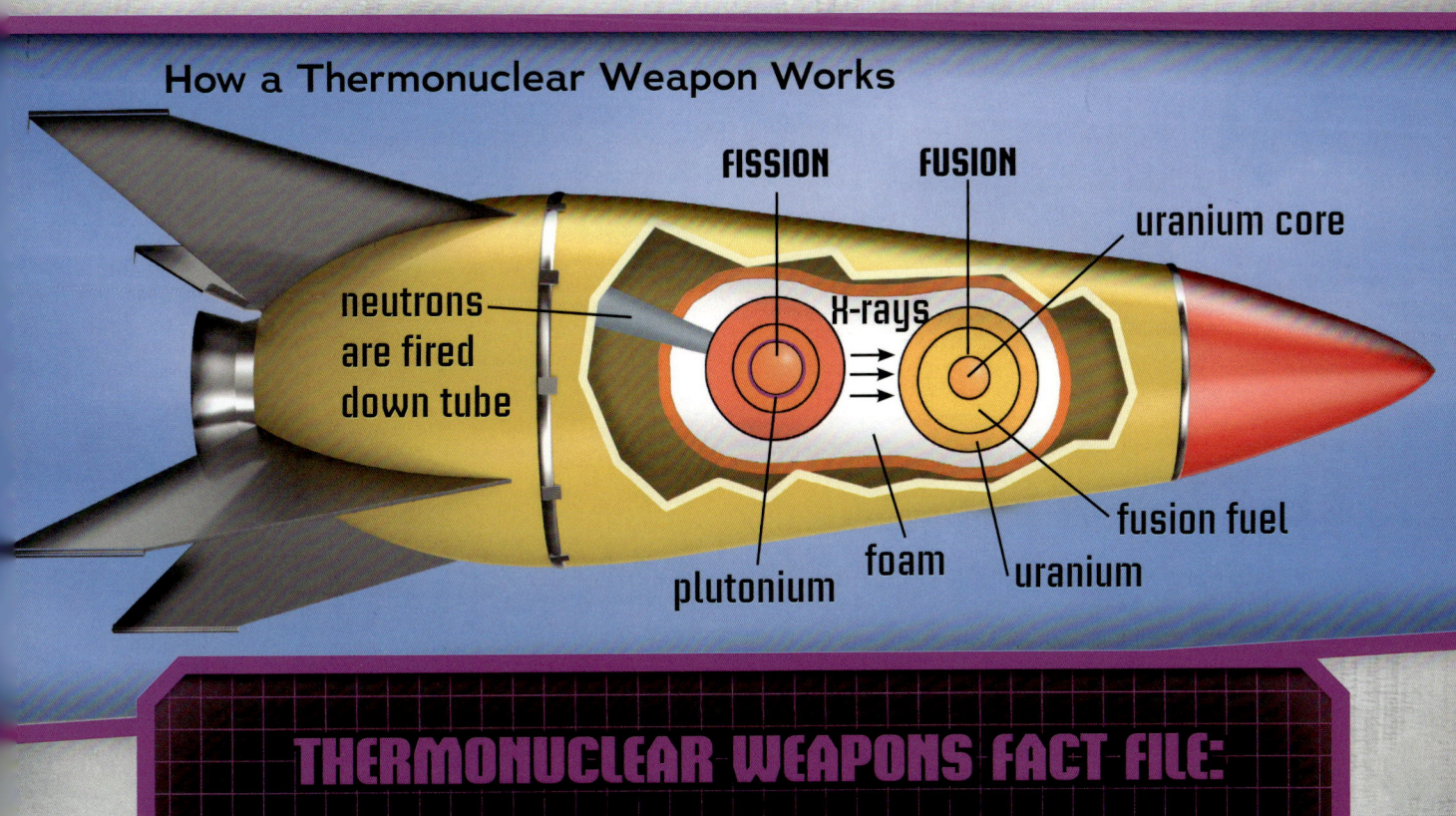

FISSION OR FUSION?: Thermonuclear weapons work by using fission to trigger a fusion reaction

HOW DOES IT WORK: A neutron is fired into the uranium or plutonium, which sets off a nuclear fission reaction. This causes a fusion reaction in the warhead.

HIROSHIMA

On the morning of August 6, 1945, a U.S. B-29 bomber, the *Enola Gay*, dropped the first atomic bomb ever used in warfare. The target was the Japanese city of Hiroshima. World War II had ended, but Japan had refused to surrender. An invasion of Japan would have cost many American lives, so the decision was made to drop the deadly bomb.

A small parachute slowed the bomb as it fell so the pilot had a chance to fly away from the area. It exploded 1,900 feet (580 m) above the ground. Between 60,000 and 80,000 people were killed instantly. Many died later from **radiation sickness**. The final death toll was around 135,000 people.

The aircraft just before their bombing mission of Hiroshima. The *Enola Gay* is on the right.

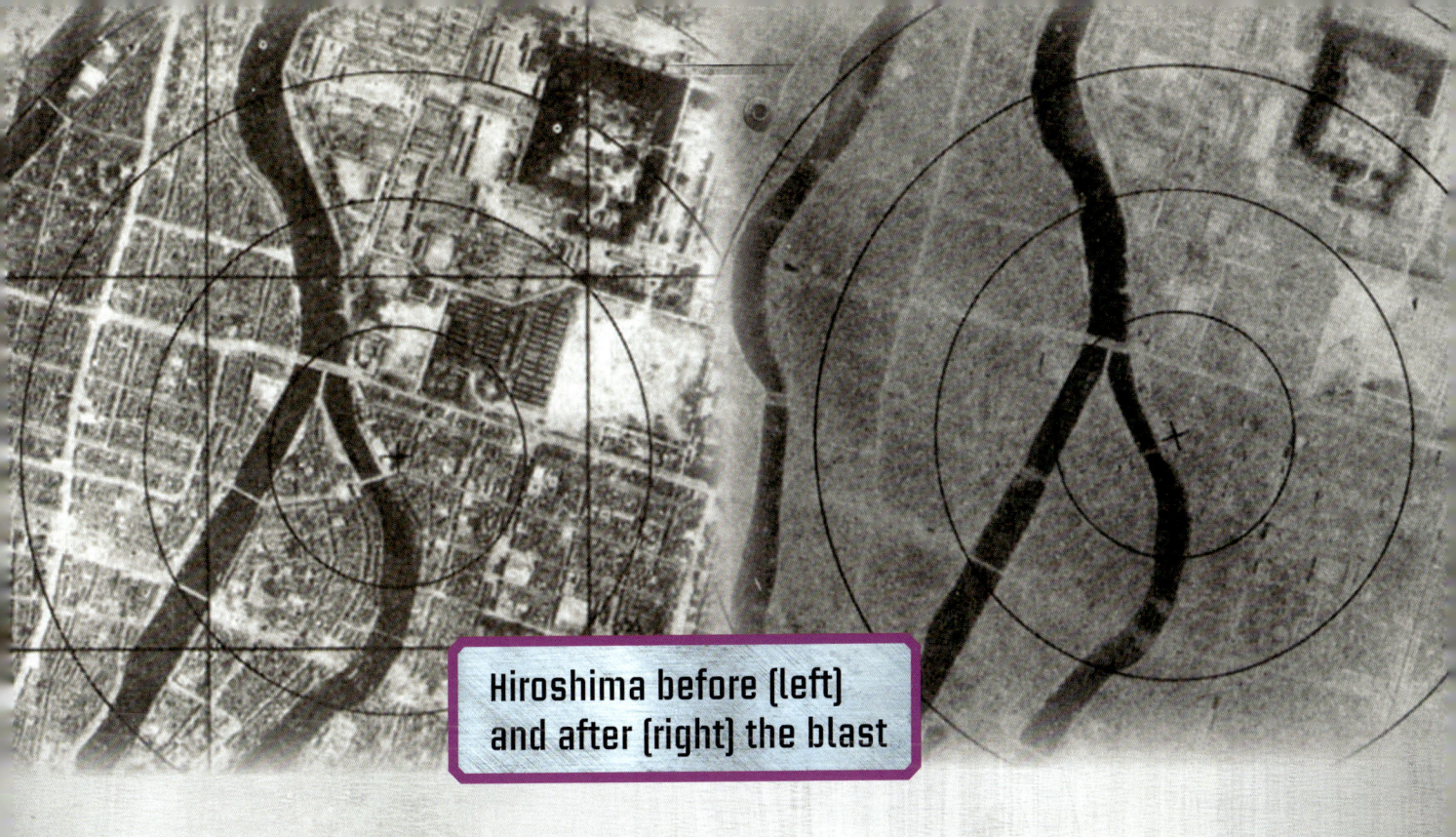

Hiroshima before (left) and after (right) the blast

The blast destroyed over six square miles (15.5 square km) of the city of Hiroshima. The heat of the explosion started fires that lasted for days, killing many of the survivors of the initial explosion. Thousands more people were made homeless.

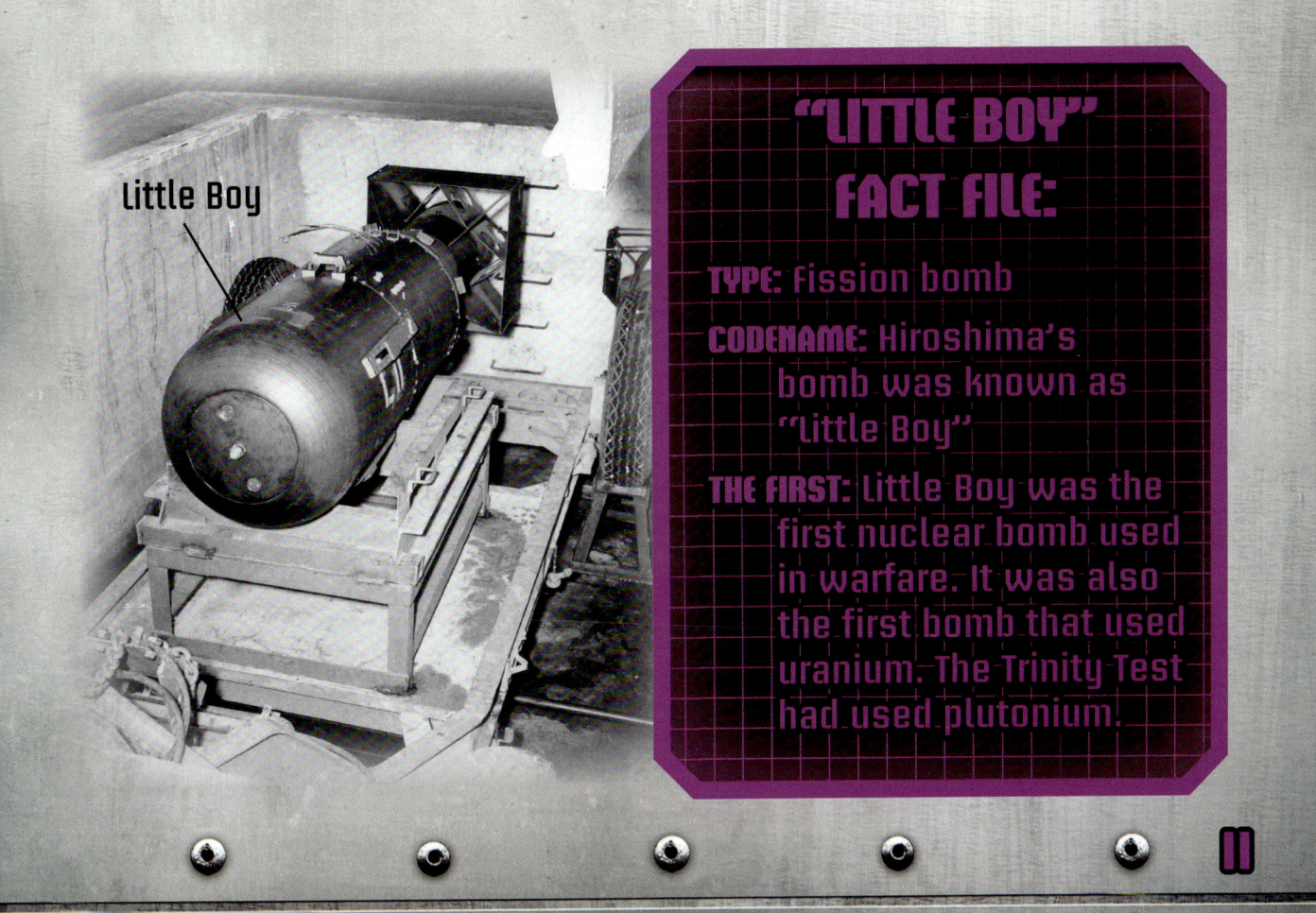

Little Boy

"LITTLE BOY" FACT FILE:

TYPE: Fission bomb

CODENAME: Hiroshima's bomb was known as "Little Boy"

THE FIRST: Little Boy was the first nuclear bomb used in warfare. It was also the first bomb that used uranium. The Trinity Test had used plutonium.

THE B-29 BOMBER

The Pacific island of Tinian, August 5, 1945, evening. The B-29 crew were told the nature of the next day's mission for the first time. The group had trained in secret. They only knew as much as necessary to do their jobs, and no more. Before that evening, only a handful of people on the project knew they were preparing to drop an atomic bomb.

The enormous B-29 bomber, the *Enola Gay*, set off early the next morning. Several hours into the flight, the weapons expert armed the gigantic bomb. Several B-29s had crashed at Tinian during takeoff. They did not want to run that risk while carrying "Little Boy."

B-29s had flown on bombing raids over Japan before, dropping conventional bombs like this one on Osaka.

This B-29 named Fifi is still flying. It was restored by aircraft enthusiast Vic Agather, and named after his wife.

The B-29 Superfortress was larger and faster than its predecessor, the B-17 Flying Fortress. It could fly higher and further, and carry a larger bombload, too. It was one of the most advanced airplanes of World War II. The B-29 had guns that could be fired by remote control. Two **pressurized** crew areas at the front and back were connected by a long tube over the bomb bays. Crew members could crawl along the tube between the areas. The tail gunner also had a separate pressurized area.

B-29 SUPERFORTRESS FACT FILE:

USES: The B-29 was used as a long-range, high altitude heavy bomber

HOW HIGH?: The B-29 could fly at altitudes up to 31,850 feet (9,710 m). Few enemy aircraft could reach that height.

HOW FAST?: The B-29 could fly at speeds of up to 350 mph (560 km/h). The combination of its height and speed meant it was almost impossible to catch.

NAGASAKI

Three days after the bombing of Hiroshima, another B-29 armed with an atomic bomb headed out across the Pacific. The target for this mission was the city of Kokura, home to one of the largest weapon stores still standing in Japan. That day Kokura was covered by clouds. The B-29 turned south and went instead to bomb Nagasaki.

The cloud may have been caused by bad weather, but some believe the Japanese created a smokescreen when they saw the bombers approaching. The smoke also may have been haze from a previous nearby bombing. Whatever caused it, the clouds saved Kokura, but led to the devastation of the port of Nagasaki.

The *Bockscar* and its crew, who dropped the atomic bomb on Nagasaki

The crews of both B-29s that dropped the atomic bombs over Japan have said they felt sure what they did was right. Even though the bombs led to many deaths, they felt a longer war would have led to many more. It must have been a terrible burden to live with, however.

"FAT MAN" FACT FILE:

TYPE: Mark IV atomic fusion bomb

CODENAME: Nagasaki's bomb was known as "Fat Man" because of its shape. It got its name from a character in the film "The Maltese Falcon."

THE LAST: "Fat Man" is the last nuclear weapon to have been used in warfare to date.

After the bombing, *Bockscar* was dangerously low on fuel due to a faulty fuel pump. Instead of landing as planned at Iwo Jima, it tried to land at Okinawa. It couldn't warn the airfield as its radio wasn't working. With only enough fuel for one landing attempt, *Bockscar* landed at dangerously high speed, firing distress flares. The heavy B-29 veered toward a row of parked B-24 bombers. The pilots managed to regain control, and by standing on the brakes, they swerved at the end of the runway and finally came safely to a stop!

THE COLD WAR

The Cold War was a period of political and military tension between the Western **democracies** and the **communist** countries of Eastern Europe. The Cold War occurred after World War II, between 1947 and 1991. The two sides never directly fought each other. Instead, both sides armed themselves in the fear that there would be an all-out nuclear world war.

Each side had nuclear weapons. This fact meant that neither side wanted to attack the other, as such an attack would lead to the total destruction of the attacker. This situation led to a kind of peace.

The city of Berlin in Germany was split down the middle by a wall. The wall divided the Eastern communist side from the Western side. Many people died trying to cross the wall.

The Berlin Wall that separated West and East Berlin.

Nuclear bunkers were built to house military leaders in case of a nuclear attack. The bunker pictured below in Cheyenne Mountain, Colorado, houses a command center for NORAD, the North American Aerospace Defense Command.

Nuclear war almost broke out during the Cold War. In 1979, at NORAD, someone accidentally ran a training tape which simulated a nuclear attack. Aircraft took to the sky armed with nuclear warheads. Luckily someone realized the mistake just in time!

The 25-ton blast doors that protect the NORAD bunker

It may seem strange to spend money making weapons that no one ever uses. It costs a lot of money to produce nuclear weapons. It is perhaps a cost worth paying if it keeps the world at peace.

BROKEN ARROW

A "broken arrow" is what the U.S. military call an accident that involves nuclear weapons. In February 1950, a B-36B Peacemaker bomber crashed in Canada. Before it crashed it **jettisoned** a Mark IV atomic bomb. This accident was the first ever "broken arrow."

The B-36 flew out from Alaska. Its mission was to practice a nuclear attack on San Francisco to test whether the B-36 could operate during a cold, Russian winter. Its bomb contained deadly uranium and 5,000 pounds of explosives. The cold did affect the aircraft. Seven hours into the flight, three of the six engines had to be shut down, and the other three engines were failing.

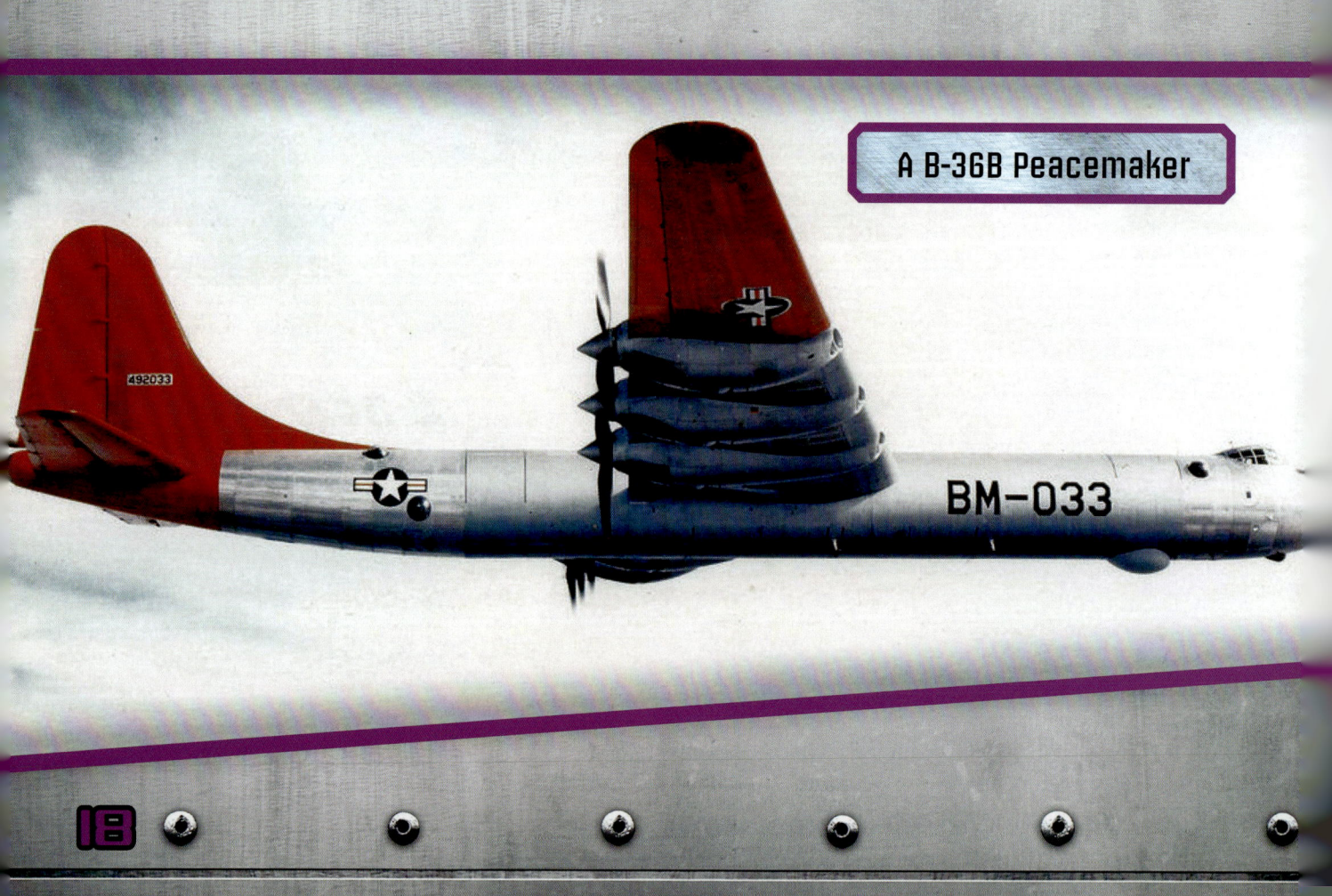

A B-36B Peacemaker

The crew decided to abandon the aircraft. The bomb was jettisoned and exploded in midair. The crew bailed out and the commander set the autopilot to crash the plane into the open ocean. Twelve of the 17 crew were found alive. The aircraft was never searched for, because it was believed to be at the bottom of the Pacific.

Ted Schreier

> In 1953, crews searching for a missing millionaire found the wreckage on a mountain in British Columbia! One theory is that Ted Schreier, the weapons officer, may have remained onboard and taken control of the aircraft. He was a pilot, but had never flown anything as large as the B-36. His body has never been found.

In 1954, a USAF search crew reached the B-36 and removed anything they did not want to fall into enemy hands. They removed the crash-proof container the bomb's core was carried in. They were also said to have removed a body bag, although that was never confirmed. They then destroyed the wreckage using grenades.

TESTING TIMES

To develop any sort of weapon, the ideas must be tested. That becomes very difficult when the weapon you are testing is as deadly as an atom bomb. Finding a safe place to practice using such a bomb is very difficult.

Scientists Stanislaw Ulam and Edward Teller worked on designing the first fusion bombs. The U.S. had captured the Enewetak Atoll, in the Pacific Ocean, from Japan. That seemed like an ideal place to test their ideas. The people that lived there were moved off the islands. On November 1, 1952, the first bomb test was detonated. Code named "Ivy Mike," it was over 450 times more powerful than the bomb dropped on Nagasaki.

The Ivy Mike test

IVY MIKE FACT FILE:

TYPE: Fusion bomb

DELIVERY METHOD: Ivy Mike was detonated remotely from a control ship, *Estes*

APPEARANCE: The 82-ton "Mike" device was essentially a building. It looked more like a factory than a weapon!

STRENGTH: Mike's blast was as powerful as all the bombs dropped on Germany and Japan during World War II

Ivy Mike crater

Castle Mike crater

Enewetak Atoll

The Ivy Mike test at Enewetak Atoll completely vaporized one of its islands, Elugelab. The explosion left just a crater behind. This satellite image shows the Ivy Mike crater (left) and another crater from a later test named Castle Mike, to its right.

FALLOUT

Nuclear fallout is the leftover radioactive material in the atmosphere following a nuclear blast. It is called that because it "falls out" of the sky after the explosion. During a nuclear explosion any matter vaporized in the fireball absorbs neutrons from the explosion and becomes radioactive. When this material is absorbed in rainclouds it forms a deadly radioactive dust which falls to Earth.

A cloud made from radioactive material after an underwater nuclear test in the Pacific Ocean

FALLOUT FACT FILE:

WHY IS IT DANGEROUS?: Fallout from a nuclear explosion can cause radiation sickness

HOW DOES IT SPREAD?: When a nuclear bomb hits the ground it sends up dust. The radioactive cloud of dust can be carried by the wind a great distance and radioactive matter can enter the water and food supplies.

In the 1960s, when people were fearful of a nuclear war, many built fallout shelters. A fallout shelter is designed to protect from harmful fallout until radioactivity has fallen to a safer level.

Many public shelters were built by governments. Individuals built them in their own homes, too. In Switzerland, buildings built since the 1960s must by law have a fallout shelter. They have enough shelters for the whole population, plus room for 10 percent more!

In the U.S., the government built public fallout shelters, located by signs like the one above. The family shelter pictured below was built in the front yard of a house in Indiana. The family kept it stocked and ready to move into at a moment's notice.

TSAR BOMBA

On October 30, 1961, the Soviet Union tested the largest nuclear weapon ever detonated over some islands in northern Russia. It was named Tsar Bomba, which means "King of Bombs." In July 1961, the Soviet leader Nikita Khrushchev asked for a bomb to be created that could be detonated during a Communist Party Congress held that October. The development team had little time to prepare the bomb.

It created a very small amount of fallout, considering its size. It was designed like this as most of the fallout would have fallen on Soviet territory.

TSAR BOMBA FACT FILE:

TYPE: Thermonuclear weapon

HOW LARGE WAS TSAR BOMBA?: Tsar Bomba weighed 27 tons! It was designed to hold 100 megatons of explosive, but actually only held half that. That was because of fears about the amount of fallout.

STRENGTH: The bomb was 1,400 times as powerful as the Hiroshima and Nagasaki bombs combined

A Tu-95 "Russian Bear" aircraft that was modified to carry Tsar Bomba

The huge size and weight of the bomb caused problems. The Soviet bomber chosen to deliver the bomb was the Tu-95. Tsar Bomba weighed two and a half times the Tu-95 aircraft's normal weapon load. The Tu-95 had to be modified. The heavy bomb doors were removed.

A parachute was attached to Tsar Bomba to slow the bomb as it fell. This gave the pilot, Andrei Durnovtsev, just enough time to get a safe distance away before the bomb exploded. The time between releasing the bomb and it exploding was just 188 seconds.

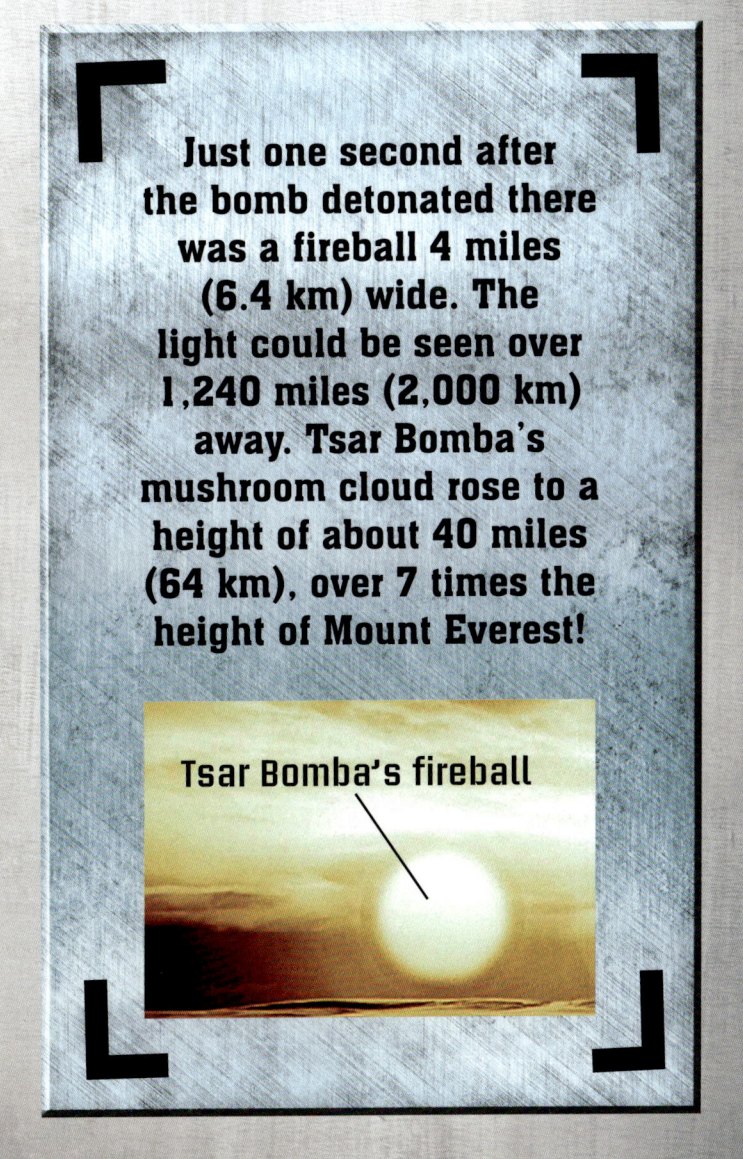

Just one second after the bomb detonated there was a fireball 4 miles (6.4 km) wide. The light could be seen over 1,240 miles (2,000 km) away. Tsar Bomba's mushroom cloud rose to a height of about 40 miles (64 km), over 7 times the height of Mount Everest!

Tsar Bomba's fireball

TRIDENT MISSILE

Many modern missiles now have nuclear warheads. The Trident missile is launched from a submarine. The missile is powered in three stages by three different rockets, a little like some spacecraft are. Trident has a guidance system which can be programmed to direct it to its target. Once in the air it also has a clever system that uses the position of the stars to fine-tune the missile's flightpath. Trident can carry up to 12 nuclear warheads. It has a range of up to 7,500 miles (12,000 km) and is very accurate!

TRIDENT FACT FILE:

TYPE: Submarine-launched missile

WARHEAD: Trident is armed with thermonuclear warheads. Their power is about eight times the strength of the bomb dropped on Hiroshima.

COST: Each Trident missile costs around 100 million dollars to build. That includes the missile and its launch system.

The USS *Ohio* carries Trident missiles

Trident is launched from underwater. Trident submarines are fitted with special launch tubes. The pressure of expanding gas in the launch tube forces the missile out and to the ocean surface. Once the missile is far enough from the submarine, the first of the three-stage motors fires. A spike then appears out of the nose of the Trident to cut any air drag!

Weapons are expensive to produce and many governments are under pressure to stop spending money on them. This sculpture at a music festival is campaigning to scrap Trident. Many people believe the money spent on nuclear weapons would be better spent helping people.

NUCLEAR CLEANUP

After a nuclear event, radiation can **contaminate** everything. Most contamination can be removed by simply wiping the surface with a cloth. Some radiation may need harsher removal techniques, such as using chemicals. Some buildings may even need the surface layer of concrete removed!

Most communities have a radiation disaster plan. Officials are on hand to help if such an emergency occurs. Most recommend you stay inside, in a room with the fewest windows. This is because the walls can block some of the harmful radiation.

It is important to detect where radiation occurs so that treatment of an area can be targeted to the right places. Special detectors can scan to see if there is any radiation. These soldiers are using detectors to scan radiation levels in the soil during a simulated attack. Soldiers are constantly training to hone their skills in case of a nuclear attack.

People carrying out decontamination need to wear special protective suits. The suits are sealed with tape at the seams, and arm and leg holes, to prevent any contamination getting on their skin. The suits often include breathing apparatus.

HUMAN DECONTAMINATION FACT FILE:

1: Remove outer clothing and place it in a sealed bag

2: Survey the whole body for radiation. Using a marker, mark any areas where contamination is high.

3: Using warm water and soap, wash the body. Cold water closes the pores, trapping radioactive contamination in the skin. Hot water creates steam which may mean contamination is breathed in.

4: Repeat until the contamination is at a safe level

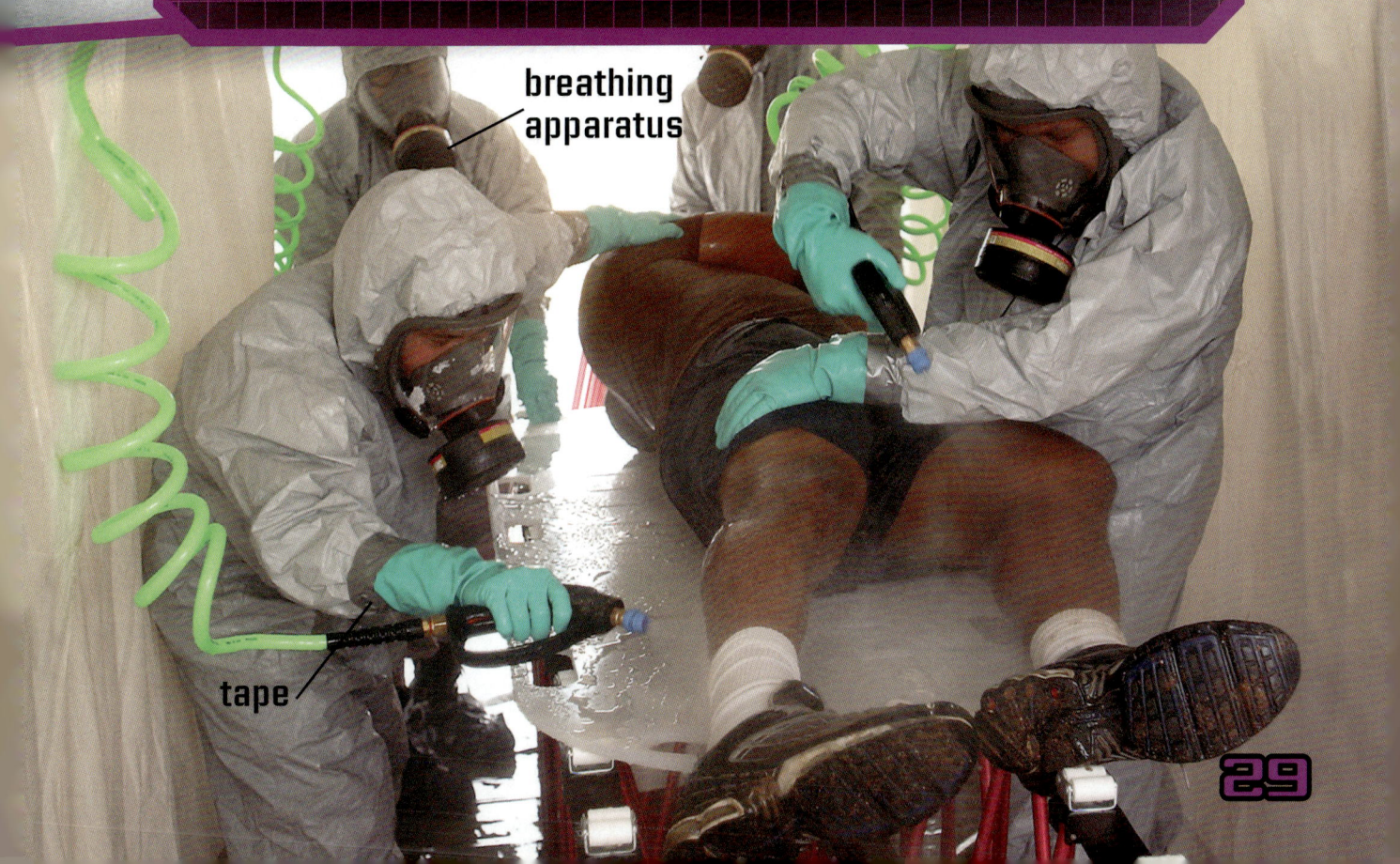

breathing apparatus

tape

GLOSSARY

atom: The smallest particle of an element that has the properties of the element and can exist either alone or in combination.

communist: Following a social system in which property and goods are shared.

contaminate: To make impure or unfit for use by adding something harmful or unpleasant.

conventional: Standard and in relatively wide use. In the case of weapons; not nuclear, biological, or chemical.

democracies: Countries governed by the people.

detonation: To cause to explode with sudden violence.

jettisoned: Thrown or dropped from an aircraft or ship.

neutron: An atomic particle that is present in all atomic nuclei except hydrogen.

nuclear energy: Energy involving a nuclear reaction.

plutonium: A radioactive metallic element.

pressurized: Have a near-normal atmospheric pressure.

radiation: Giving off radiant energy.

radiation sickness: Illness caused by exposure to radiation.

radioactive: Giving off rays of energy or particles.

simulated: Imitated.

terrorist: A person who illegally scares or threatens with violence.

thermonuclear: Transformations in the nucleus of atoms of low atomic weight that require a very high temperature.

tungsten carbide: A hard gray compound made by the reaction of tungsten and carbon at high temperatures.

unstable: Readily changing in chemical composition or physical state or properties.

uranium: A silvery heavy radioactive metallic element.

FOR MORE INFORMATION

BOOKS

Bearce, Stephanie. *The Cold War: Secrets, Special Missions, and Hidden Facts about the CIA, KGB, and MI6 (Top Secret Files of History)*. Austin, TX: Prufrock Press, 2015.

Moore, Sandra. *The Peace Tree from Hiroshima: The Little Bonsai with a Big Story*. North Clarendon, VT: Tuttle Publishing, 2015.

Morimoto, Junko. *My Hiroshima*. Melbourne, Australia: Lothian Children's Books, 2014.

Due to the changing nature of Internet links, PowerKids Press has developed an online list of websites related to the subject of this book. This site is updated regularly. Please use this link to access the list:
www.powerkidslinks.com/thtw/nuclear

INDEX

Agather, Vic 13
atoms 4, 8, 9

B-17 bomber 13
B-29 bomber 10, 12, 13, 14, 15
B-36B bomber 18, 19
Berlin, Germany 16
Bockscar 14, 15
broken arrow 18, 19

Castle Mike 21
Cheyenne Mountain, Colorado 17
Cold War, the 16, 17

Durnovtsev, Andrei 25

Elugelab 21
Enewetak Atoll 20, 21
Enola Gay 10, 12
Estes 21

fallout 22, 23, 24
Fat Man 15
Fifi 13
fission 4, 8, 9
fusion 4, 8, 9, 20, 21

Gadget, the 7
Groves, Leslie, Lt. Gen. 7

Hiroshima, Japan 4, 10, 11, 14, 24

Ivy Mike 20, 21

Kokura, Japan 14
Khrushchev, Nikita 24

Little Boy 11, 12
Los Alamos, New Mexico 6

Manhattan Project, the 6, 7
Mark IV atomic bomb 15, 18

Nagasaki, Japan 4, 14, 15, 20, 24
neutrons 8, 9
NORAD 17

Ohio, USS 27
Oppenheimer, J. Robert 7

plutonium 6, 8, 9, 11

radiation 6, 10, 28, 29
radiation sickness 10, 22
radioactive 22, 23, 29

Schreier, Ted 19

Teller, Edward 20
thermonuclear weapons 8, 9, 24
Tinian 12
Trident missile 26, 27
Trinity 7
Tsar Bomba 24, 25
Tu-95 bomber 25
tungsten carbide 6

Ulam, Stanislaw 20
University of California, Berkeley 7
uranium 8, 9, 11, 18

World War II 4, 7, 10, 16, 21